ZAIN THE EAGLE

A Story of City, Nature, and Renewal

J. R. Arinwood

PART I-The Arrival

CHAPTER 1
The Market Stirs

2

The market always woke before the city admitted it was morning.

Crates scraped against concrete. Canvas awnings sighed open.

Someone laughed too loudly near the coffee cart, the sound rising like steam and then vanishing. Mango Street smelled of citrus and bread and metal warming under a pale sun.

Marla stacked oranges in careful pyramids, her fingers already cold. She had worked this corner long enough to feel the day before it happened. Tuesdays moved slowly. Thursdays rushed. This morning felt…paused.

A shadow crossed the stalls.

It wasn't sudden. It didn't dart or flicker. It moved the way a thought does when it insists on being finished.

Marla looked up.

The market quieted in pieces. A voice stopped mid-sentence. A knife rested against wood. A child froze with a coin clenched in his fist

.Above them, wings opened.

Zain.

He glided low, broad and unhurried, white head catching the thin gold of early light. The air shifted around him, as if the street itself leaned back to make room. He circled once, reading the currents, and dipped again—close enough that Marla could see the dark seam of feathers along his wing.

Phones appeared. Someone gasped. Someone else laughed, unsure why.

"A bird," a man said, already lifting his camera.

But Asha—small, quiet, sketchbook hugged to her chest—didn't move. She watched the curve of the wings, the steadiness of the glide, the way the shadow stitched itself across the awnings.

"It's an eagle," she whispered.

The word traveled. It changed shape as it went.

Zain rose on a slow breath of air and turned east. The market exhaled.

When sound returned, it came in waves.

Marla didn't look away until he was gone.

CHAPTER 2
A Name Takes Hold

By noon, the video had a title.

Eagle Over Mango Street.

By evening, it had a thousand opinions.

Lena watched it loop on her phone while the bus lurched towards downtown. The clip was shaky, the frame too wide, the moment too brief. Still—there it was. The wings. The glide. The way the market fell quietly before anyone thought to be impressed.

She replayed it without sound.

Eagles didn't come here. Not anymore. The river was too far, the rooftops too loud, the sky too busy with things that moved faster than memory.

At home, Asha spread her pencils across the kitchen table. She drew the market first—boxes, signs, faces tipped upward. Then she drew the wings. She erased. Drew again. Erased less.

Her mother watched from the doorway.

"What's his name?" she asked, gently.

Asha didn't answer right away. She shaded the curve of the beak, the line of the brow. She pressed the pencil harder where the wing caught light.

"Zain," she said finally.

"Zain?" Her mother smiled. "Why Zain?"

Asha shrugged. "It fits."

The word left the room and didn't come back.

By morning, the name had found a thousand mouths.

Radio hosts said it carefully, testing the sound. A chalk scrawl appeared on the sidewalk near the market—*Zain was here*. Someone taped a sign to a lamppost with a sketch that looked suspiciously like Asha's.

When Zain returned, the crowd was waiting.

He came from the north this time, riding a higher line of air. Cameras tilted up in unison. Someone cheered. Someone else cried.

Above all, indifferent to names and noise, Zain traced the sky as if it had always been his.

CHAPTER 3
Lines in the Air

The first meeting was standing room only.

City Hall smelled like paper and impatience. Microphones hummed. A projector blinked awake and cast a map onto the wall—streets, parcels, thin green outlines where green still existed.

The Mayor adjusted his tie.

"We are monitoring the situation," he said, and the word *situation* did too much work. "There is no immediate cause for alarm."

Lena sat near the back, notebook open. She wrote *situation* and underlined it. She wrote *Zain the Eagle* and circled it.

Across the room, a developer cleared his throat. "With respect," he said, "an isolated sighting does not constitute a policy shift."

Outside, the sky darkened with weather. Inside, voices rose.

Asha listened from the steps, legs swinging, eyes on the ceiling as if she could see through it. She imagined the air above the building—the invisible lines Zain followed, the routes no map could hold.

When the meeting ended, nothing had changed on paper.

But the city had begun to draw itself differently.

That night, Zain crossed the river at dusk, wings cutting a clean path through violet light. He passed over rooftops and rails and the soft square of the market, now closed and dark.

Somewhere below, a child pressed her palm to glass and looked up.

CHAPTER 4
The City Watches Back

At 7:42 a.m., Zain lifted from the rooftop of the post office.

The movement was economical—one beat, then another—and suddenly the city was below him, arranged into angles and alleys and slow veins of traffic. From this height, Brandon looked composed, almost kind. Noise flattened. Urgency softened.

A delivery driver caught the moment by accident. The phone tilted late; the frame missed the first wingbeat. Still, it was enough.

By the time Zain crossed the courthouse dome, the video had found an audience. By noon, it had found a narrative.

Lena stood on the sidewalk with her camera lowered, watching the sky instead. She felt the tug of her job—capture it, explain it, give it shape—but something in the steadiness of his glide resisted translation.

Zain didn't linger. He never did. He traced a line, tested the air, and moved on.

Below, the city began to keep score.

CHAPTER 5

A Question of Space

The plans had been approved months ago.

Renderings showed glass and green roofs, smiling figures walking dogs where trees were scheduled to arrive later. The language was careful—*revitalization, mixed-use, future-forward*—and no one had objected loudly enough to matter.

Until now.

"An eagle doesn't need a permit," Marla said to anyone who would listen. She handed over change and shook her head. "The sky didn't ask us."

At City Hall, the map returned to the wall. Someone added a dot. Someone else added a line.

"Habitual presence," a consultant said, tapping the screen. "If it's established."

"How long does that take?" the Mayor asked.

Outside, Zain passed overhead, unseen by those arguing his coordinates.

Asha watched from the steps, sketchbook open, drawing lines that curved where the map stayed straight. She drew the wind the way it felt, not the way it was measured.

That night, rain arrived without apology. Zain rode it easily.

PART II The Movement

CHAPTER 6
Signals

The first sign appeared on a cardboard box.

SAVE ZAIN.

It leaned against a bus stop, ink bleeding where the rain had found it. By morning, there were three more. By afternoon, a dozen.

Lena interviewed a teacher who spoke carefully about balance. She spoke to a contractor who spoke about jobs. She spoke to a teenager who said nothing and held up a drawing instead.

At dusk, a crowd gathered where no crowd was scheduled to be. Someone brought a flashlight. Someone else brought a drum. Children chalked wings across the pavement.

They didn't chant at first. They waited.

Zain arrived as the light failed.

He crossed the square in a clean arc, wings catching the last of the day. Flashlights tilted up, then steadied. The drum stopped.

For a moment, the city listened to itself.

When the chant finally rose, it carried a name that had already begun to mean more than a bird.

Zain.

Zain the Eagle.

He did not circle. He did not descend. He passed through the light and into the dark, leaving behind a city that knew it had crossed a line it could not uncross.

CHAPTER 7
Feathers and Flashlights

The square was filled without instruction.

People arrived at the clusters after work, after dinner, after the news. Some carried signs printed neatly at home. Others wrote in marker on cardboard torn from boxes. Children brought chalk and colored the pavement with wings that overlapped and blurred.

Flashlights came out as the sky dimmed. Someone counted down without knowing why.

Lena moved through the edges, recording faces. Not statements, faces. The way mouths set when a chant paused. The way hands lifted when the light shifted. She caught herself looking up more than down.

When Zain appeared, it was not dramatic. He slid into the glow like a thought finishing itself. The lights found him and held.

The chant rose then, steady and unforced.

"Zain".
"Zain".
"Zain the Eagle".

He passed once above the square, wings wide enough to quiet the drum. For a breath, the city forgot to film. Then the moment scattered into a thousand screens.

Zain didn't slow. He never did.

But the square stayed full long after he was gone.

CHAPTER 8
The Feed

By morning, the name trended.

Clips looped with captions that argued with each other. Experts weighed in. Comment sections grew teeth. Someone sold shirts by noon. Someone else called the police by dusk.

The Mayor's office released a statement that said nothing and said it twice.

Lena watched the feed scroll past her coffee. She wrote, then deleted, then wrote again. Facts were easy. Meaning was not.

At school, Asha's teacher asked the class to write about the sky. Asha drew instead—Zain mid-glide, the city smaller than it liked to be.

On the river bridge, a banner appeared overnight. It stretched white and wide:

LOOK UP.

Traffic slowed. Horns sounded, unsure.

Above it all, Zain traced routes no algorithm could predict. He passed through frames and out of them, leaving the feed to chase what it could not hold.

PART III- Legacy

CHAPTER 9
Lines Are Drawn

The meeting spilled into the hallway.

Voices sharpened. Someone pounded a fist against a door that did not open faster. A lawyer spoke about precedent. An activist spoke about memory. The words collided and slid past each other.

Outside, the square filled again.

Police stood at the edges, hands visible, faces neutral. Parents kept children close. Someone handed out water.

When Zain came, the sky was bruised with cloud.

He flew low this time, close enough that the rush of air reached the crowd. Signs lifted. Flashlights steadied. The chant rose, not louder than before, but clearer.

Zain the Eagle.

Across the street, a developer watched from behind glass. On the steps, Asha held her drawing against her chest like a promise.

Zain crossed the square and climbed into the weather. The city did not follow. It stood where it was and realized that the line had already been drawn—not in ink or law, but in the air it shared.

CHAPTER 10

The Edge of the Forest

The decision arrived quietly.

Not with applause or press cameras, but with a notice taped to a door and an amended map uploaded after midnight. The green outline widened by a careful margin. The language softened. A hearing was postponed.

People noticed the next morning when the trucks didn't arrive.

At the edge of the North Ridge, volunteers cleared debris by hand. Someone brought coffee. Someone else brought seedlings wrapped in damp newspaper. Children knelt and pressed roots into soil that smelled like rain and promise.

They argued briefly about a name. Then they didn't.

"This is Zain's Haven," Asha said, as if reporting a fact already agreed upon.

No one corrected her.

At golden hour, Zain circled the clearing once—wide, attentive—then lifted into a higher line of air. The forest took a breath it hadn't known it was holding.

CHAPTER 11

What Remains

The city learned new habits.

People paused at crosswalks and looked up. Teachers opened windows. Vendors planted herbs in cans and set them where sun could reach. The river path filled again, not all at once, but steadily.

Lena filed her piece late. She kept the facts lean and let the space between sentences do some of the work. It ran on the front page without a photo.

At the market, Marla added a small sign beneath the oranges—*Look up again*—and smiled when customers did.

Zain came and went. Sometimes weeks passed without a sighting. Sometimes he crossed the skyline twice in a day, as if checking the city's posture.

The arguments didn't vanish. They shifted. They learned to listen.

At dusk, Asha closed her sketchbook and left it closed.

CHAPTER 12
The Sky Remembers

Years later, people told the story differently.

Some said Zain stayed. Some said he moved on. Some insisted they saw him still, a flash of white at the tree line when the light turned honest.

Asha, grown now, stood with a child of her own at the edge of the Haven. The trees were taller. The air was cooler. The city hummed at a distance it had learned to keep.

"Did he save the city?" the child asked.

Asha smiled. She waited for the wind to finish what it was saying.

"No," she said. "He reminded it."

Above them, a shape crossed the open blue—unhurried, exact. Whether it was Zain or another eagle hardly mattered. The city lifted its face the same way.

And the sky, patient as ever, remembered.

www.ingramcontent.com/pod-product-compliance
Lightning Source LLC
Chambersburg PA
CBHW020609130626
46552CB00007B/3113